Helen Orme taught for many years before giving up teaching to write full-time. At the last count she had written over 70 books.

She writes both fiction and non-fiction, but at present is concentrating on fiction for older readers.

Helen also runs writing workshops for children and courses for teachers in both primary and secondary schools.

How many have you read?

Two years on:

Secrets

 Helen Orme

Ransom

Secrets

by Helen Orme
Illustrated by Chris Askham

Published by Ransom Publishing Ltd.
Radley House, 8 St. Cross Road, Winchester, Hampshire
SO23 9HX, UK
www.ransom.co.uk

ISBN   978 184167 743 9

First published in 2011
Copyright © 2011 Ransom Publishing Ltd.

Illustrations copyright © 2011 Chris Askham

A CIP catalogue record of this book is available from the British Library.

The rights of Helen Orme to be identified as the author and of Chris Askham to be identified as the illustrator of this Work have been asserted by them in accordance with sections 77 and 78 of the Copyright, Design and Patents Act 1988.

4

Meet the Sisters ...

Siti and her friends are really close. So close she calls them her Sisters. They've been mates for ever, and most of the time they are closer than her real family.

Siti is the leader – the one who always knows what to do – but Kelly, Lu, Donna and Rachel have their own lives to lead as well.

Still, there's no one you can talk to, no one you can rely on, like your best mates. Right?

1

Eddie

Donna had a day off school.

'Do you want to come shopping?' asked Briony. 'Or are you going out with the Sisters?'

The Sisters were Donna's friends.

'No,' she said. 'I'd like to come out with my real sister instead.'

It was busy in the shopping centre. Briony dragged Donna from one shop to another.

'Can't we go and have a coffee?' Donna begged. 'I need to sit down.'

They were lucky. The coffee shop was crowded, but Briony saw a gang of her friends.

'Come on,' she said. 'We'll sit with Paula and Emma.'

They squeezed in round the table. Donna knew some of Briony's friends, but there was one guy she hadn't seen before.

He saw her looking at him and grinned at her.

'Who are you then?' he asked. 'Are you mates with Bri?'

'She's my sister.'

Donna looked at Briony. She was busy talking to Paula. 'My name's Donna,' she said. 'What's yours?'

'Eddie.'

Donna smiled at Eddie. She thought he was really nice. They were getting on well until Briony decided it was time to hit the shops again.

'Come round with me instead,' said Eddie.

Donna thought about it. 'Better not,' she said. 'Briony will only moan.'

'How about meeting when she's not around?'

'O.K. Give me your mobile.' Donna put in her number. 'Call me.'

'Come on Donna – we need to get on,' said Briony. Donna turned and smiled at Eddie.

'See you,' she said.

2

'I've met this guy ...'

Donna was really pleased when Eddie texted. 'Meet 2morrow?'

The next day was Saturday. She was going riding but she really wanted to see him again. She texted back, 'Coffee shop 4.30'.

She asked Briony what Eddie was like.

'He's good fun, but he can be a bit mad. Be careful, O.K.?'

On Saturday morning even riding couldn't take her mind off Eddie. She told Mrs Samways she had to get home early. She wanted to shower and get changed before she met him.

Briony was right. Eddie was good fun to be with. And he wanted to see her the next day. She was supposed to be meeting the Sisters, but they wouldn't mind.

She rang Siti.

'Can't make it – sorry.'

'What's up – is everything O.K.? You sound funny.' Siti sounded worried.

'No, it's cool. It's just that I've met this guy ...'

'Oh! Well, have fun – tell us everything tomorrow!'

On Sunday Eddie took her ice skating. Donna loved it. Then they met up with some of his friends and went off in a crowd. Donna knew some of them – they went to college with Briony. They usually treated her like a kid but now she felt like part of the gang.

At school the next day she told the Sisters about him. 'You're going to be busy,' said Siti. 'How are you going to fit us in as well as Eddie and your riding?'

'Don't worry,' said Donna. 'I'll always have time for you lot.'

3

In love

Donna was in trouble. She hadn't done her homework.

'You've had plenty of time to get it done,' Mrs Williams said. 'Come on Donna. This is no time to give up on your work. Is it your riding?'

Donna blushed. She didn't like being told off.

'Sorry,' she said.

As soon as Mrs Williams let her go,
Donna rushed off. The Sisters had waited for
her but she just waved at them as she ran by.

'See you,' she yelled, but she didn't stop.

'I'm worried about her,' said Kelly.

'She's in love,' said Siti.

'Yeah, I know, but she's never been like this before.'

'She's even missed some riding lessons,' said Lu. 'She told me she might give them up.'

'She can't do that!' said Rachel. 'She's much too good!'

The Sisters weren't the only ones who were worried. Briony was too.

'Just be careful,' she told Donna. 'Remember what I said. Don't let him get you into things you can't get out of.'

'It's cool, don't worry. I can handle it.'

4

'It's my decision'

School had finished and Siti went to find her dad.

'Sorry Siti, I can't come yet,' he said. 'Do you want to go home on the bus instead?'

'No,' laughed Siti. 'You just want to get out of buying me that new CD you promised. I'll wait, then we can still get to the store before we go home.'

'Do you want to wait in my office?'

'No, you're O.K.,' she said. 'I'll go back to the form room and do some homework. Come and find me when you've finished.'

When she got back to the form room she was surprised to see Donna.

'Hi,' she said, looking hard at Donna. 'Are you all right?'

Donna shrugged her shoulders. 'Suppose so.'

'Do you want to talk about it?'

'It's Eddie.'

'Has he dumped you?'

'No, it's not that. But I'm worried that if I don't, you know …'

'He wants sex?'

Donna nodded.

'Will he dump you if you don't?'

Donna nodded again.

'Do you want to?'

'Yeah, but …'

'It's a big 'but' isn't it?' said Siti. 'Think of all the things that could go wrong.'

'I know. I'm not stupid!'

'What have you said to him?'

'I told him I need more time, but he says I need to grow up. He says everyone else does it.'

'Have you told Briony?' asked Siti.

'No way!'

Siti put her arm round Donna. 'Talk to us,' she said. 'We'll help.'

'I know.' Donna pushed Siti away. 'But it's my decision, isn't it?'

5

As bad as parents

Siti wasn't happy. The next day she talked to the others.

'If she was O.K. with it she wouldn't be talking about it,' she said.

'But she does like him a lot,' said Rachel. 'Nothing's ever got this far before.'

'What can we do?' asked Lu.

They all tried to talk to Donna.

'How many girls has he been with?' Kelly asked her. 'What if you catch something?'

'What if you get pregnant?' said Lu. 'What would your mum and dad say?'

But Donna's answer was always the same.

'I know what I'm doing. Eddie says he'll take care of everything.'

Donna was getting fed up with the Sisters.

'Leave it!' she told Siti. 'It's nothing to do with you lot.'

'But we're worried,' said Siti. 'It's only because we care about you.'

'Yeah, well, so does Eddie, and I love him.'

'We've got to lay off,' Siti told the others. 'If we keep on at her she's more likely to do it. She says talking to us is as bad as talking to parents!'

Then Donna told them something that really worried them.

'His mum and dad are going away next weekend. He'll be at home by himself!'

6

News

The Sisters knew what Donna meant.

'She's going to do it, isn't she?' said Lu. 'How can we stop her?'

'Tell Briony,' suggested Rachel.

'We can't do that,' said Siti. 'She'd never forgive us.'

Then Kelly came in with some news. 'I've been talking to Jamie,' she said.

'You haven't told him, have you?' asked
Rachel. 'He might let on to Briony.'

'No, of course not,' said Kelly crossly. 'But
even if I had, my brother's not that stupid.'

'What did he say?' asked Siti.

'He said that he thinks Eddie's got some girl pregnant!'

They were all shocked. It was a minute before anyone spoke.

'But Donna said she hadn't done it with him.'

'I told her to be careful!'

'What are we going to do?'

'How does Jamie know anyway?' asked Siti.

'He said Briony told him.'

Siti pulled a face. 'Donna's not going to keep it secret for long.'

The next morning they were waiting for Donna to get to school. 'Are we going to tell her what we know?' asked Lu.

'No,' said Kelly 'We'd better wait till she tells us.'

'Just be 'specially nice to her,' said Siti.

But Donna didn't come into school.

Siti sent a text at break but Donna didn't answer.

'We'd better go round after school,' said Siti. 'We can't leave her on her own.'

At the end of the day they went round to Donna's. Siti rang the doorbell.

Michael, Donna's little brother, opened the door.

'She's not very well,' he said. 'She's in her bedroom.'

They went upstairs. Siti knocked on the door.

'Go away,' shouted Donna. 'I don't want anything.'

Siti opened the door gently.

'It's us,' she said. Donna burst into tears. They all went in and Lu shut the door.

'Have you told your mum yet?' asked Rachel.

'Told her what?'

'About Eddie; about being, you know ...'

Donna dried her eyes. She stared at them. 'Why should I tell them? They didn't like him anyway. They're really pleased.'

'What are you talking about?' asked Siti. 'How can they be pleased?'

Donna shook her head. 'Look,' she said. 'I don't suppose you know. Briony only told me yesterday. He's dumped me. But only 'cos I couldn't dump him first. He's been seeing someone else. That girl Emma. And he's got her pregnant.'

'Emma! So you're not ...' But Kelly saw Siti glaring at her and stopped speaking. Donna burst into tears again.

'He was seeing her all the time. He only went out with me for what he could get. I'm never going to trust a boy again.'

Kelly put her arms round Donna. She looked at the others.

'But you can always trust us,' she said.